For my dear and helpful daughters
Abigail, Jennifer, and Amanda
(and special thanks to
Ann D. and Amy E.)

First published 1995 by Walker Books Ltd
87 Vauxhall Walk, London SE11 5HJ

This edition published 1996

10 9 8 7 6 5 4 3

© 1995 Marylin Hafner

This book has been typeset in Bembo.

Printed in Hong Kong

British Library Cataloguing in Publication Data
A catalogue record for this book is available
from the British Library.

ISBN 0-7445-4722-9

THIS WALKER BOOK BELONGS TO:

_____

MUMS DON'T GET SICK!

Marylin Hafner

WALKER BOOKS
AND SUBSIDIARIES
LONDON • BOSTON • SYDNEY

SATURDAY! NO SCHOOL! SCRAMBLED EGGS!

AND BACON!

Saturday was a special day at Abby's house. She didn't have to rush to school, and Mum and Dad were not at work.

But this Saturday when Abby woke up, something seemed different.

Abby went into Mum's room.

Then she got dressed and went downstairs.

After breakfast, Dad had to go to the shops.

Next, Abby put a wash on.

Sarah came to the door.

Abby managed to get the wet clothes into the dryer … but David was soaking and the floor was flooded.

She put David into dry clothes.

Dad heated Mum's special soup and Abby made ham sandwiches for lunch.

Then they all went upstairs to help Mum get ready for lunch.

MORE WALKER PAPERBACKS
For You to Enjoy

A YEAR WITH MOLLY AND EMMETT
by Marylin Hafner

Molly's good friend is a fluffy orange cat called Emmett. Together they share
holiday and birthday times, summer times and winter times,
good times and funny times.

0-7445-6015-2   £4.99

GRANDAD'S MAGIC
by Bob Graham

Grandad's magic may not be big magic, but it's large enough
to cause a stir in Alison's house one Sunday lunchtime!

"Full of neat asides and significant details… Excellent."
The Times Educational Supplement

0-7445-1471-1   £3.99

NOT A WORRY IN THE WORLD
by Marcia Williams

"A brilliant book… Marcia Williams illustrates in a very funny cartoon-strip style…
She also offers a few solutions, but one of the best is to laugh
at your own fears – something this book will help children do."
Tony Bradman, Parents

0-7445-2375-3   £4.50